I AM
TUCKER,
DETECTION
EXPERT

I AM TUCKER,

DETECTION EXPERT

Catherine Stier

**illustrated by
Francesca Rosa**

Albert Whitman & Company
Chicago, Illinois

To Jill, a friend to every pup she meets at the airport (and everywhere else). Thank you for being my book-recommendation-sharing, always caring, "true-blue" friend too. —CS

To my talented grandparents, thank you for your art and your love. —FR

Library of Congress Cataloging-in-Publication data
is on file with the publisher.
Text copyright © 2021 by Catherine Stier
Illustrations copyright © 2021 by Albert Whitman & Company
Illustrations by Francesca Rosa
First published in the United States of America
in 2021 by Albert Whitman & Company
ISBN 978-0-8075-1678-2 (hardcover)
ISBN 978-0-8075-1685-0 (ebook)

Printed in the United States of America
10 9 8 7 6 5 4 3 2 1 LB 24 23 22 21 20

Design by Valerie Hernández

For more information about Albert Whitman & Company,
visit our website at www.albertwhitman.com.

Contents

Chapter 1

On the Job

I know my mission, and I'm ready.

I'm cruising through the airport when I spy a woman wearing sunglasses waiting by the luggage carousel. She carries a flowery bag that gives off a scent I can't ignore. As I get closer, I lunge forward and give the bag a big sniff, just to be sure.

Bingo!

One whiff tells me she's bringing something into the country that she shouldn't. I can't let that happen. I do my supersecret signal to alert my partner that I've found something. What's my signal? Simple—I sit.

Just then, the woman looks down and sees me. I give her my most serious look. Saving the world is important business, after all.

"Oh, hello, cute little doggy!" she says.

Sigh.

I get that all the time. I gotta say, it isn't easy being so adorable. I mean, superheroes aren't supposed to be cute. We're heroic!

Reggie, my human partner, gets my signal and takes over.

"Excuse me, do you have any food items in your bag?" he asks the woman.

She fumbles in her bag and pulls out the dangerous object I smelled—an orange.

"Only this," she says.

I give that orange a fierce glare. It may look innocent, but some people don't realize how much harm a piece of fruit can do! Reggie

knows though. After giving me my doggy treat reward, he takes the orange. "Good job, Tucker," he tells me. Then he politely tells the woman why some fruits, meats, and other foods can't be brought into the country.

"These products might carry insects or diseases that could cause a lot of damage to forests or the food grown on farms," he says.

The woman looks surprised. "I didn't know,"

she says. "I forgot I tossed that in my bag. I'm sorry."

Reggie gives the woman a friendly smile. He reminds her to declare any food brought into the country. Then he sets the orange aside to be disposed of later. After that, we move on, and I'm back to work, doing what I do best. It's the perfect job for a beagle like me.

What's my job exactly? Let me explain.

One thing everyone learns two minutes after meeting me is that I love food. All kinds of food, anytime, anyplace. Some might think my love for food is my biggest flaw. They'd be wrong.

In fact, it's just the thing that makes me so good at my job. I work as a kind of food finder, also known as a detector dog. I'm one of four other beagle detector dogs at this airport. Together, we're called the Beagle Brigade.

Reggie says the dogs of the Beagle Brigade have everything a true superhero team has:

✓ Cool outfits? Yep. Each of us has a spiffy official jacket to wear.

✓ Superpowers? Definitely. We are amazing sniffers and scent finders.

✓ Team members working together to save the planet? That's us!

✓ And crime-fighting partners? Absolutely! Just like Batman has Robin, each dog works alongside a human partner. My partner is Canine Officer Reggie.

Best of all, we have an important mission. Like Reggie told the woman with the orange, we protect the country's forests and farms. I know about forests. They're amazing woodsy places and home to animals like deer and raccoons. As for farms, that's where food comes from— and, well, you know how I feel about food.

As the incoming passengers head out, Reggie glances at a clock. "Break time, Tucker," he says.

Just before we leave the international arrivals area—that's where people come in from other countries—we pass by a poster. It has a picture of my fellow Beagle Brigade member

Ruby. Along with Ruby's photo, the poster has crossed-out pictures of things that shouldn't be brought into the country, like plants and meat and fruit. Ruby has been with the Beagle Brigade for many years. She's sniffed out more stuff than any other dog on our team. I am still pretty new. But I hope one day to be just like her.

Reggie and I move on to the main part of the airport. It's a big, busy place, with shops and restaurants. Reggie stops a moment to greet his friend Jay, who works at the airport too. As I watch the travelers hurry by, I catch a few of Reggie's words. "Tucker will be leaving early," I hear him say. "Another team is taking over this afternoon."

Leaving early? Another team? This is news to me. Am I being taken off the job?

Okay, I know I'm not perfect. Even with our super noses and all our training, no detector dog is right every time. Like earlier today, I thought I smelled an apple in a backpack, but after I gave Reggie my supersecret signal, he didn't find anything inside.

It happens. Still, I hope I'm not being replaced because of a couple mistakes.

Let me prove myself, Reggie! I think. *I know I'm still new, but I'll show you I can be as good as Ruby someday.*

I'm so eager, I act before I think. Reggie's friend Jay is carrying a crumpled paper bag. It gives off a strong scent of something I was trained to detect.

I scamper to the bag and press my nose against it to get a better whiff.

Bingo!

I guess I've surprised Jay, because the bag slips from his hand and hits the ground. A cheeseburger rolls out, pops out of its wrapping, and falls cheese-side down onto the floor.

Proudly, I give the alert. I sit and look up at Reggie.

See Reggie, I was right! I think. *I know beef when I smell it.*

But instead of giving me a doggy treat, Reggie frowns.

Oops.

I think I've just made another mistake.

Chapter 2

Super from the Start

"No, Tucker!" Reggie groans. "You're off duty now. This isn't the arrivals area."

Sorry, Reggie.

Reggie's friend Jay looks at the messy burger and the ketchup splattered on the airport floor.

"Aw, Tucker, that was my lunch," Jay says. "And I promise, it was safe. I bought that cheeseburger right here at the airport."

I guess that means no doggy treat for me.

Reggie scoops up the cheeseburger and buys Jay a new lunch.

"Come on, Tucker," Reggie says finally. "Let's get you outside."

We head to a fenced-in outdoor space. Reggie says there are areas in the airport reserved for people with important jobs. Well, this place is specially designed for us detector dogs.

As we arrive, I see Atlas, a Belgian Malinois, leaving with his human partner. Bigger dogs like Atlas work as detector dogs here at the airport, too, but with different programs. I guess they're trained to sniff out other things, because they leave the food finding to us beagles. Atlas looks big and tough and serious as he heads back to work. Like a real canine superhero.

Once we're inside the fence, Reggie takes off

the leash and my jacket. I nose around some small shrubs before doing my business.

The cool breeze feels great as it blows back my floppy ears. Still, even on my break, I can't help wondering why we're leaving early today. And I worry. I remember another time when something didn't work out because of mistakes I made.

You see, I haven't always worked with Reggie and the Beagle Brigade. Like most superhero stories, the tale of my life has a few bumps along the way.

Everything was awesome in the beginning. When I was eight weeks old, a kind human named Edward adopted me, and my little puppy paws were set on an exciting new path.

"Since I'm retired, I've got time for new hobbies," Edward told his niece Melissa when he introduced us. "I think someday this pup and I might explore the dog show world."

"He's so sweet," Melissa said as she lifted me up for a kiss. "What's his name?"

"I mostly call him Tucker. He likes to tuck himself in small spaces, like under the coffee table. But I found out purebred show dogs can also have fun, out-of-the-ordinary names. So this pup has an official purebred name too."

That's when I learned that like some superheroes, I have another name. It's kind of like my secret identity!

"May I present Barker True-Blue Tuckberry," Edward said.

Pretty fancy, huh?

"My, that is a big name for a little dog!" Melissa said with a laugh. "Well, Uncle Edward, I have a gift for you and Mr. Barker True-Blue Tuckberry." And she gave us a sparkly doggy brush.

Sometime later, Edward and I started getting ready for dog shows. A dog show, I learned, is a kind of contest for dogs. To be a winner, a dog must look and act the part of a well-groomed, well-trained pup. I figured if Edward was excited about this dog show stuff, I'd give it a try.

Each day, Edward would brush my fur with the sparkly brush. It felt like the best back scratch in the world! Then we'd begin training. My favorite part was the agility course. I learned to jump over hurdles and scramble through tunnels. I even practiced running across a moving seesaw Edward set up in our backyard. I was super speedy!

I was almost two years old when Edward entered me in our first dog show.

Let's just say, things didn't go quite as expected.

On the big day, Edward brushed my coat until it gleamed. For the first event, he led me into the ring, and I showed off my glossy fur, bright eyes, and good manners before the judges and the crowd. Turns out, though, I wasn't very interested in prancing around a ring. After just a few steps, I dashed off to impress everyone with my amazing super-speed. Somehow I tangled my leash around Edward's leg right in front of the judges.

Oops.

Later that day, I was ready to wow everyone at the dog show's agility course.

Things started off great. I sailed over the

first hurdle and through a hoop like a champ. The audience cheered! But as I scampered to the top of the seesaw, my superpowered nose caught a scent. When the seesaw swayed to the ground, I jumped off and darted away. My nose pulled me toward the audience, seeking that irresistible aroma—beef jerky, I think it was.

The crowd roared with laughter when, instead of finishing the course, I tried to climb into the stands to hunt down that smell.

Edward was laughing too as he scooped me up.

"Well, Barker True-Blue Tuckberry, I don't think dog shows are right for us," he said. "But this big world is filled with opportunities. We'll find something else. Something we'll both love to do."

And we did.

Chapter 3

A New Skill

A few days after the dog show, Edward had a bad day. I could tell because he used his gloomy voice.

"The sink drain is clogged, I spilled juice on the rug, and it's storming outside, so we can't go to the park. What else could go wrong?" he grumbled.

Somehow I knew just what to do. I scurried

from my spot under the coffee table. I sat right in front of Edward.

Don't be sad, Edward. We can hang out together inside today, I thought. I stared at him till he gave me a pat. Pretty soon, Edward was smiling again.

"Barker True-Blue Tuckberry, you really are a loyal, true-blue friend. And you sure have a talent for perking someone up. That's got me thinking. How would you like to train for a new job helping people?" he asked.

Ahroooo! I gave my happy little howl. *I really like people, Edward! Almost as much as I like food.*

"Well, I have an idea," he said.

First, Edward taught me a few new commands. He also brought me to the park and to friends' homes, where I visited with

22

humans of all ages.

Then one day, Edward drove us to a building. There was a sign in front with a picture of a dog.

What's this all about? I wondered.

When we walked inside, a woman welcomed us. "I know you've been working at home with Tucker. Learning to be a therapy dog team is like basic training for many different volunteer jobs. If Tucker passes today's evaluation, we will offer you an assignment wherever the need is greatest," she said. "Some therapy dog teams visit hospital patients. Others go to colleges to help students relax before their big tests. And lots of libraries bring in friendly dogs to listen to kids read."

"Those all sound great, don't they, Tucker?" Edward asked.

Anything we do together is fun, Edward! I thought.

At my evaluation, lots of interesting things happened. I proved that I wasn't shy around crutches or wheelchairs and that loud noises didn't startle me much. I showed that I understood commands and liked being with people too. I'd learned so much training with Edward for dog shows that everything was a snap.

"Tucker passed with flying colors," the office lady said afterward. "And we have your first assignment. You'll greet travelers as part of Furry Friends for Flyers, a program just starting at the airport. How does that sound?"

Okay, I guess, I thought. *But what's an airport?*

I learned soon enough.

Before we left for our new job, Edward tidied me up with the sparkly brush. Then he put on my uniform—a bright bandanna that tied around my neck.

The airport was a big, loud place with lots of humans rushing about and airplanes parked outside the giant windows.

Who knew airplanes were that huge? I thought. *They look so tiny in the sky!*

Although I was working at the airport, I wasn't part of the Beagle Brigade then. I had a different job. "As a Furry Friends for Flyers team, you'll greet people so they feel less stressed on a busy travel day," a program leader told us. She patted my head. "Tucker, you just need to be your sweet self."

Just be myself? No sweat. I can do that! I thought.

That day, I met a little boy bouncing with excitement. "I'm going to Florida to see my grandma," he told me. Later, a team of young humans in matching jackets surrounded me. I could sense their good mood. "Hey, little doggy, give us a high five! We're on our way to the championship game," one girl said. I held

up my paw and wagged my tail for good luck.

But not everyone we met was in high spirits.

"I'm a bit nervous," one man told Edward. "Truth is, I've never flown before." I sat with the man until boarding time and felt him grow calmer.

"Our shift is almost over," Edward said finally. "But we have time for one more stop. Let's see if there are any soldiers at the USO room."

There we met a young woman wearing tan and green, waiting for her next flight. Her eyes lit up when she saw me.

"He reminds me of my dog," she told Edward. "Tuffy is staying with my parents while I'm deployed, and I miss him already." She sat right down next to me. "Hey, Tucker, can I visit with you for a while?"

Yes, I'd like that! I thought. I snuggled close and tucked my nose under her arm.

"Now I see why you're called Tucker," she said. Seeing that soldier smile was the best! And I began to think helping people feel better might be a special kind of a superpower too.

Even as a therapy dog, though, I sometimes

made mistakes. I remember once, we were called to the airport for what Edward called a "Welcome Home to Our Military" event. A few Furry Friends for Flyers dogs showed up—me, a collie, and a French bulldog.

A group of soldiers came forward, looking happy to be home. Edward and the other humans cheered. Families waved signs. One little boy standing next to me held a plate of cookies to welcome his dad. They smelled heavenly! I'm only canine—how could I resist? Quick as a wink, I grabbed one.

Edward was even quicker. Before I could gobble that cookie, Edward snatched it away.

"No, Tucker! Remember your manners!"

I dropped my head till my ears flopped forward.

Sorry, Edward.

I saw the collie and the bulldog staring at me. I guess they weren't tempted by the cookies like I was.

Edward had me shake my paw with the boy to apologize.

"Oh, Tucker, don't let that nose of yours get you in trouble," Edward told me quietly. "Not only was that rude, but chocolate chips can make you sick. And you know I want you to be safe and healthy."

That's what I remember most about Edward. Even when I made mistakes, he still loved me.

And I miss him.

Chapter 4

Restless Days

Edward and I always had fun together. We went for walks, visited dog parks, and watched shows on a big screen in his living room. That's how I learned about superheroes! And twice each week, we strolled through the airport. As a Furry Friends for Flyers dog, I met pilots, flight attendants, airport workers, and lots of excited—and sometimes worried—travelers.

I didn't quite know what happened when people walked through those special doors to the airplanes, but I know it scared some humans!

"You have a knack for sniffing out those who need you most and cheering them up," Edward once told me after I got a grumpy toddler to laugh. "And guess what? I read a scientific study that found therapy dogs not only help people, but doing their job seems to make those dogs happy too."

Scientific study? I don't know what that is, I thought. But I thumped my tail at Edward's smile.

Pretty soon, though, things changed.

We were home one afternoon when Edward called out, "Just running errands, Tucker. Be back soon."

But Edward wasn't back soon. I tucked myself under the coffee table to wait. Outside, the sky

grew dark. As the evening wore on, I crept to the window. I needed to get outside and find a tree. It was getting urgent!

Just when I couldn't hold it a moment longer, the front door opened. A woman I knew walked in.

"Sorry you were alone so long, Tucker," Melissa said.

I ran to the back door.

No time for chitchat, human! Please let me outside fast!

I made it just in time.

After I came back inside, I watched Melissa gather my things—my dog bowl, dog food, leash, and my favorite back-scratching sparkly brush. There was a scent of worry about her. Something was up.

"Uncle Edward is at the hospital, so you're coming home with me, Tucker. I'm going to take care of you for a while," Melissa said. And that's what she did.

Melissa's apartment was nice, but there wasn't much for a dog like me to do. She'd leave early and be back midday for a quick walk. Then she'd come home at night and start making phone calls.

I heard the words "Uncle Edward" and

"emergency surgery" and "recovery time" a lot during those calls. Sometimes I heard my name too. One night, Melissa set her phone down and began to cry. I rested my head on her hand.

What's wrong, human?

She let out a long breath.

"Oh, Tucker, the good news is Uncle Edward is getting better," Melissa said. "He's moving from the hospital to a place where he can rest and recover. But he can't take care of you now." She smoothed my ear. "I know you're restless

here. I'm gone so much, and I'll have to travel for work soon. I just can't seem to find a good home for an energetic beagle like you." Then she smiled through her tears. "But I'll figure something out. I promise."

I felt bad for Melissa, but she was right. I was restless.

I missed being busy.

I missed my important job at the airport and all the people I met there.

Most of all, I missed Edward.

True to her word, though, Melissa came through for me.

"Well, Tucker, I have a plan," she said one evening. "I talked with Uncle Edward, and he thinks it's perfect for you. We'll start things rolling on Saturday."

Later that week, Melissa drove us to her friend

Annie's house. We went into the backyard, and Annie brought her camera phone.

"I was so excited to read there's a need for beagles to work as detector dogs at airports," Melissa explained to Annie. "Tucker would be great! He's smart, full of energy, and loves airports. We just have to record an audition video to show the detector dog center he's right for their program."

I didn't know what an audition was. Still, after being cooped up in Melissa's apartment, I was glad to be outside in Annie's yard. But Melissa was doing some pretty silly things! While Annie worked the camera, Melissa popped open an umbrella. It wasn't even raining! She dropped a clipboard that landed with a bang on the patio. Both times, I just looked up at her.

You're acting strange, human, I thought.

"That's a good sign!" Melissa told Annie. "He wasn't startled by sudden movements or sounds. Now this next test shows whether Tucker has the strong food drive needed for this job."

That's when things got fun! Melissa hid a treat under a magazine on the patio.

I found it right away! She threw a handful of treats into the grass—and I hunted down and gobbled up each one.

We even drove to a pet store, where I strutted through the opening doors.

"That proves Tucker's not afraid of automatic doors. And that's a wrap," Melissa said when we finished. "I'll send this to the National Detector Dog Center. Everyone cross your fingers and paws that this works!"

I still remember the day Melissa burst through the door with the news.

"I just got word—you've been accepted, Tucker! You're going to train to be a detector dog for the Beagle Brigade. Just think of it! If all goes well, you'll be working at an airport again."

I was excited because Melissa was excited. But I had lots of questions too.

What's a Beagle Brigade? Where am I going? What will I be doing? I wondered. *And will this new job be the one that sticks?*

Chapter 5

Hero in Training

Soon Melissa brought me to the airport for my very first plane flight. Honestly, I don't know why some people worry about flying. It was kind of fun and tickled my tummy a little bit.

After the plane landed, I was brought to a place with lots of buildings and outdoor spaces. At first, I was distracted by the new sights, smells, and sounds. There were lots of other dogs there too! But it didn't take long for me to settle in.

My days at this new place were busy and challenging. They were a welcome break after the quiet and sometimes lonely times at Melissa's place.

I started each morning running, playing fetch, and kicking up my heels with a human

called a trainer. Then the lessons began.

On the first day, a trainer told me, "Tucker, we're going to help you hone those amazing, scent-finding superpowers of yours."

And she did! Over time, I learned to identify five special smells: beef, pork, mango, apple, and citrus—things like oranges and lemons. I knew those were the smells they wanted me to sniff out because whenever I got a whiff of one and gave my supersecret alert, I got a treat!

The trickiest part, though, was learning to *not* alert to other foods, like chewing gum and chocolate. I was such a food fan, I wanted to sniff out all the yummies. But I soon learned that if I alerted to the wrong scent, no matter how tempting, I didn't earn myself a treat.

One memorable day, some new humans showed up. We dogs were brought out to visit with different people all afternoon. I got some friendly hellos and ear scratches from lots of interesting folks. Reggie, though, was special. He spoke to me in a kind, friendly way like Edward did. I liked him right away.

Reggie must have felt the same. From that

day on, we were partners and continued training as a team. I learned to understand and trust Reggie, and he figured out how to read my alerts and signals. He even knew when I needed a break. I guess reading my mind is Reggie's superpower.

Each day we worked together on what Reggie called "training exercises." I had another name for them: games! Like, sometimes, there would be a room full of plain cardboard boxes. The rules were simple: I'd sniff each box one by one. When I hit upon one of those big-five special smells—*Bingo!*—I'd give my alert. Then I'd look at Reggie, waiting for my treat and a "great job, Tucker." On another day, we checked out a row of cloth bags that all looked the same.

We played these games a lot. Humans sure

seem to love hiding things inside of other things.

My favorite was when we inspected a row of luggage. That was the most challenging search, since the suitcases were made of thicker materials and came in all shapes and sizes. Still,

time after time, I'd pass my snout close to the luggage to locate which ones had the hidden food. I got better and better at these games until, I admit, I was pretty much a pro.

The months of training ended with a final detector test for each dog-and-human team.

For those who aced the test—like Reggie and me—there was a graduation ceremony. At my graduation, I got my official detector dog jacket.

Then came the big surprise. Reggie and I boarded a plane and arrived somewhere very familiar.

Hey, I know this place! I thought.

It was *my* airport, the one where Edward and I had volunteered as a Furry Friends for Flyers team.

That's how I came to be working here today.

Chapter 6
A Good Place to Be

I finish my outdoor break, and Reggie replaces my jacket and leash. Together, we make our way back to the international arrivals area. It's been a month since we began working as a Beagle Brigade team, and every day brings something new. Right now we're passing a woman on a small stage. She's strumming a guitar and singing a cheery tune for the passing airport workers and travelers. I see Reggie nodding his head with the music.

That's one of the reasons I love working here. Since the day I first stepped a paw into this airport, there's always been lots going on!

I remember one snowy day when Edward and I were here for our Furry Friends for Flyers work. I didn't know why the airport was even more crowded than usual. Plus, the terminals and shops were decked out with ribbons and giant candles. There were big tree-looking things that didn't smell like real trees at all. A group of people stood on the small stage, singing songs and jingling bells. I saw a guy go by wearing what looked like antlers on his head.

You can't fool me, mister, I thought. *A dog with hunting instincts like mine knows you are no deer!*

"It's a shame that flights will be delayed with all these folks trying to get home for the holidays," Edward said to another volunteer as they looked at the crowds.

Outside, I could see heavy snow pelting the big glass windows and covering the runway.

Just then, a voice spoke over the loudspeaker. "Well, merrymakers, it looks like the flight to

Dallas is delayed two hours," a man said.

People groaned.

"So let's have an old-fashioned paper airplane race while you wait. We gate agents will pass out paper. Let's see which budding engineers can fold up the plane that flies the farthest."

Soon little paper planes filled the air, some gliding gracefully and others crashing to the

floor. The once grumbling people were now laughing and cheering. One paper plane really soared, arcing up high and flying farther than any other. It landed right by my paws.

"We have a winner!" the voice on the loudspeaker said. Other humans hooted and clapped.

"That's mine!" A little girl cheered as she ran toward her paper plane. "It flew and flew

and flew!" She knelt and hugged me. "See that, doggy? I won!" I couldn't help but feel happy.

Now, as Reggie and I head into the international arrivals area, I see again the Beagle Brigade poster with our team's best detector dog, Ruby. Ruby's lucky. She's kept her job for years.

Then I remember what Reggie said about leaving early and another team replacing us tonight. I know Reggie and I make a great team. But Edward and I were a great team too. I can't help wondering—will I get to stay here at this airport, doing what I love? Will my partnership with Reggie and this great new job last?

Chapter 7
An Old Friend

Back at the international arrivals area, a woman in uniform, Paulette, greets us. I've heard Reggie call her the manager, whatever that is. I guess it means she helps him learn on the job.

"How's our team's newest dog doing today?" she asks.

"I have high hopes for this little guy. But we did have a slight mishap with someone's fast-food order," Reggie says.

I duck my head as he explains.

Aw, Reggie, did you have to tell her about the cheeseburger? I think.

"We're heading back out," Reggie says. "Let's see what we can do." I feel Paulette's eyes on me as I walk past the baggage carousel.

It's not long before I catch a whiff of something. A sweet, sharp scent coming from a young woman's roller bag makes me stop. I trot forward and take another sniff.

Maybe I can't think clearly, knowing Paulette is watching me, but the scent confuses me for a moment. It smells a bit like citrus. But not quite.

"Got something, Tucker?" Reggie asks.

Maybe? I think.

I hold my nose close to the roller bag, but the extra sniffs don't make things clearer.

I don't want to miss something that could be a problem. I don't want to miss the chance to earn a treat, either. So I give the alert.

"Okay, Tucker. I'll check it out," Reggie says.

After a talk with Reggie, the young woman opens her roller bag and pulls out a candle. A stinky yellow candle.

Reggie takes the candle. He chuckles when he reads the label. "'Lovely Lemon Lavender

Scented.' Well, you were close, Tucker. But it's not a real piece of fruit." He hands the candle back to the young woman. "Here you go. You may keep this. Candles are allowed," he says.

Oops again.

Paulette walks up to join us.

"False response?" she asks. Reggie nods and takes out a pen and a small notebook. I know he has to keep track of my alerts, whether I'm right or wrong. I feel bad about making mistakes. I feel even worse that Reggie's manager saw me mess up this time.

"I'm heading back to the office," Paulette says. "I'll take a look at Tucker's monthly record. Good luck, you two."

I sigh as she leaves.

First there was the problem with the cheeseburger, and now the candle.

This hasn't been my best day.

What else could go wrong? I think.

Instead, though, my day starts to get a little brighter.

The last few travelers are leaving with their luggage when I hear my name.

"Is that you, Tucker?"

I look up at a smiling face.

A *familiar* smiling face.

My tail starts to swing back and forth.

Melissa?

Reggie looks surprised. "Is this an old friend, Tucker?" he asks.

"I'm sorry to interrupt your work," Melissa says after introducing herself to Reggie. "But could I speak with you a moment?"

"Of course," Reggie says. "How can I help?"

"Tucker was my uncle's dog. He had to let

61

him go for health reasons," Melissa says. "I heard that Tucker works at this airport now. I hoped I'd see him here after my return flight today. My uncle Edward said to give you this." She reaches in her bag and brings out something familiar.

I step forward and give the thing a sniff.

Hey, that's my old sparkly brush, I think. It sure brings back memories.

Melissa crouches down to speak to me. "Uncle Edward said you're probably missing your special brush, Tucker. He said you always looked so happy and relaxed when your fur was brushed. And you were so proud of your shiny coat afterward."

I lean close to Melissa.

"Is it okay if I hug him?" Melissa asks Reggie.

"He's on duty, but we can make an exception this once," Reggie says.

Melissa puts one arm around me.

"It's good to see you doing so well, Tucker. Uncle Edward is doing well too," she says. "He'll be so proud to learn you're still at the airport, working at this important new job. You should know this—Uncle Edward is rooting for you."

Melissa stands and speaks with Reggie for a moment before giving me one last friendly pat.

I wag my tail to say goodbye. Melissa gathers her bags and turns to leave. As I watch her go, Reggie sets the brush aside.

"It's great to see an old friend, isn't it, Tucker? Now it's back to work for us," he says.

I straighten up and lift my head.

I'd been feeling down today, worried I'd never be as good a detector dog as Ruby.

But after meeting with Melissa, I want to keep trying the best I can.

After all, Melissa called my work "important."

Reggie said he has high hopes for me.

And most of all, my good buddy Edward is rooting for me.

Chapter 8

The Wildest Scent

I tackle my next searches with a new focus. I try to be less eager. I think carefully before I alert. I want to do a good job for the humans who believe in me—Reggie, Melissa, and especially Edward. In no time, I alert to apples stuffed in a duffel bag and one neatly wrapped ham sandwich in someone's pocket. I'm feeling good about these finds. I like the treats I get too! Then the manager, Paulette, returns. She looks at me. She doesn't smile.

Uh-oh. I think. *What did she find in that report?*

Paulette turns and talks to Reggie in a low voice.

Next thing I know, Reggie and I are loading into the back seat of an airport cart. My ears blow back as Paulette speedily drives the cart along the tile floor. I guess they really want me gone—they're racing me out of here!

But that's not what happens.

"We have a special assignment for you and Tucker," Paulette says as she brakes the cart. "And it's urgent."

Wait, what?

She leads Reggie and me to an area that's closed to most people.

"We gathered these suitcases here," Paulette explains. "There's been a report that someone on this flight is bringing something illegal into the country. And time is running out."

Before me is a jumble of luggage on long carts. The crew is beginning to quickly lift the suitcases down to the ground, piece by piece.

This is different than anything I've done before. And I see Reggie's concern.

Is this a test? I wonder. *Is this my last chance to prove I've got the skills to be on the Beagle Brigade team?*

"Come on, Tucker," Reggie says. "Let's get to work."

I start at one end, letting my nose lead me. It doesn't take me long to alert to a scent inside a bright case covered with stars and moons. As Reggie moves the suitcase, it bursts open and mangoes fall to the ground.

I get a treat, but I know we're not done here. I sense that Reggie is impatient. He's looking for something else and hoping we find it soon.

We continue on, and I am nosing my way from one piece of baggage to another when something unusual gets my attention. It's a strong scent coming from a suitcase with a few

rough holes poked through the corner. The case is crowded together with other luggage. I try to clamber over the other suitcases, but they're too big. I whine in frustration.

"I think we've got something here," Reggie calls out, and a crewmember hurries to move the other bags. As soon as there's an opening,

I wiggle through to the case.

"Whoa, Tucker. Careful," Reggie says. I make a beeline for the smell. I'm lucky I'm small! I'm able to tuck myself between the pieces of luggage to get as close as I can.

The scent is not one I've been trained to find. Still, something makes me perk up and sends me diving forward for a really big sniff.

Whew, I think. *What a wild smell!*

The odor that fills my nose makes me jump back.

It's not one of the big-five smells, so it's not a scent I'm *supposed* to alert to, but something deep inside tells me this: it's the smell of a living thing, a fellow creature in distress. And then I hear it. From somewhere inside the case comes a faint scratching noise.

I see Reggie and Paulette watching me, and

I freeze for a moment. If I alert, will they see it as another mistake?

If I don't alert, what will happen to whatever is trapped inside?

It goes against my training, but I know it's the right thing to do.

I scramble out from the stacks of luggage and sit before the smelly suitcase. Then I turn and give Reggie my most serious look.

Reggie, check this suitcase out—and hurry! There's something inside that needs to get out!

Chapter 9
A Big Find

A crewmember carefully pulls the suitcase forward and lays it on the floor. Paulette opens it. Now the wild smell is stronger than ever. I strain forward, but Reggie holds me back.

Paulette pulls out a plastic box and places it gently on the ground. She lifts the lid.

"Well," she says with a sigh. "We received a tip that someone was smuggling some rare and endangered animals on this flight. And here they are."

As Reggie leans forward, I move with him and catch a glimpse of the three small creatures with hard shells, barely moving around the box.

"Baby turtles!" says Reggie. "Poor little things. What will you do with them?"

"We'll charge the owner of this suitcase

with breaking the law," Paulette says. "And we will get these turtles to a vet. After that, we'll have to arrange a safe way to get them back to their home. They were captured illegally. They should be out in the wild in their home country."

Then Paulette looks right at me. "It's lucky we found these turtles so quickly. They've already had a rough trip. These little ones might not have survived any more jostling in baggage claims," she says. To my surprise, Paulette almost smiles. "Tucker was a real hero today. This was the biggest find the Beagle Brigade has made all month. You two make quite a team."

After Paulette leaves with the turtles, Reggie kneels next to me. He's quiet for a moment. I sense that he's feeling something different now.

I'm feeling different too.

"You've always been a hero, Tucker," Reggie says at last. "But this is the first time you've rescued other living creatures in quite this way. Kind of makes you think about how important this job is, doesn't it? Kind of makes you feel good about the work we do."

Chapter 10

A Friendly Face

I notice that even after pulling off our big rescue, Reggie and I still leave early. I've been stressing about this all day. But something has changed.

What is it? I wonder.

And then it hits me.

Hey, I'm not worried anymore.

Instead, I'm proud of what I've proven I can do. My nose has led me into trouble before, it's true. But it's also what saved those turtles.

Still, I am curious about why we're leaving early and where we're going.

Reggie takes off my working jacket, and I'm led to an airport office. We are greeted there by a young man who calls himself Jack. He shows us to a back room with walls covered in framed pictures and posters. One is the poster I recognize from the airport—it's Ruby with all the crossed-out foods.

In the corner of the room, there's a platform covered with a blanket.

"So this is the new spokesdog for the Beagle Brigade program?" the young man, Jack, asks as he fiddles with the camera.

"Yep. Our former spokesdog, Ruby, is retiring. She's going home to live with her Beagle Brigade partner, Lupe, and Lupe's family now.

So Tucker here is stepping up. He's proving to be one of our best," Reggie says.

"Hello, Tucker," Jack says. "Ready for your close-up?"

I sure am!

"Give us a moment," Reggie says. He brings out the sparkly brush and smooths my fur. I settle down to enjoy that familiar back-scratchy feeling I remember. "There, Tucker, now you look your best," Reggie says as he fastens my Beagle Brigade jacket.

"Here's the plan," Jack says. "We'll take some

photos tonight of Tucker and feature them on social media and on our posters around the airport. Do you think he'll sit still for the camera?"

"I'm sure he will," Reggie says.

Reggie leads me to the platform and lifts me up. Lights shine from both sides.

All of this reminds me a bit of my show-dog days. So I sit, chin up, eyes forward. Just like a show dog. Or even better—like a superhero.

Jack laughs. "Well, he's a natural. That's the perfect pose!" he says as he works the camera.

He is adjusting the camera when somewhere in the office, I hear a knock on a door and some faraway voices.

As the voices draw nearer, I recognize one first—it sounds like Melissa.

But the second voice...

"Well, there's the famous Barker True-Blue Tuckberry," someone says from the doorway.

I haven't heard that name—my secret identity—in a long time. I stay in place on the platform, wiggling, hoping, and wishing as I turn my head…

And then I see it's true! It *is* Edward!

"I heard it's your big day! I came by to say hi," he says.

Edward looks just the same, except he's leaning on a cane now.

"Thanks for inviting us to Tucker's photo shoot this evening. Uncle Edward could hardly wait," Melissa says to Reggie.

Edward comes to the platform and puts his arm around me. "Hey, Tucker, old buddy," he says.

It's so good to see him again!

I tuck my head under his chin and howl with happiness.

Ahroooo!

"I'm glad you're doing well, my friend," Edward says as he holds me tighter. I can tell Edward is well, too, and it makes me happy. "I must say, I'm so proud of you, Tucker, and the work you do as a detector dog. And with these new posts and posters, you'll be helping in

83

another way. You'll be teaching travelers about what's safe to bring in their baggage."

I burrow my head deeper into Edward's chest.

After we've had our moment, Edward steps back.

"I promise we'll mail you a poster once they're printed," Jack tells Edward. "If you check the airport's social media, you'll be seeing Tucker there too. Now, we need a couple more photos."

Edward nods. "Show 'em what you've got, Tucker," he says. And I do.

As Jack snaps more photos, I once again strike my best superhero pose. And maybe, for the first time, I *really, truly* feel like a hero. A hero despite my small size. A hero with flaws that turned out to be superpowers. A hero with friends who cared for me, trained with me, and helped me become all I am today. And all in all, being that kind of hero—an expert sniffing superhero—feels pretty great.

When you think of airports, you might not think of dogs. But like they do in so many other places, our canine friends help us there too. Guide dogs help people who are visually impaired get to their gates on time. Therapy dogs help anxious travelers feel calmer before boarding. Others work as detector dogs, sniffing out things that don't belong. You may have seen a Belgian Malinois, like Tucker's friend Atlas, patrolling at a security checkpoint. Detector dogs of this kind work with the Transportation Security Administration (TSA) to help keep passengers safe by sniffing out illegal substances or dangerous devices.

Tucker and the Beagle Brigade protect in a different way. They work with the US Department of Agriculture (USDA) to sniff out food and other plant and animal products that could bring harmful pests and diseases into the country. Sniffing out fruits and meats might not seem as important as sniffing out weapons or dangerous substances. But there's a reason all international airports across the United States employ these dogs.

With new technology, travel around the world has

never been faster and easier. While this is great for connecting people, it can also bring pests and diseases to new places more easily. Once these are introduced into an environment, they can wipe out crops and make animals sick. Dogs like Tucker help keep this from happening.

Beagles are the perfect dogs for the job. Because they're small, they can easily get around the airport baggage claim—even tucking themselves between bags to get a good sniff when they need to. As scent hounds, they have great noses, and, like Tucker, a high food drive, which helps them find exactly what they're smelling. Not to mention, they're cute! Beagles' nonintimidating looks help people feel more comfortable as the dogs search.

But beagles aren't the only ones who do this important work. Outside of airports, larger dogs, such as terriers and Labs, search planes, post offices, ships, and other places where harmful diseases carried by plants and animal products could enter the country. Together, these USDA detector dogs work every day to keep our agriculture and environment healthy. It's a big job to take on, but that's what superheroes do!

Becoming part of the Beagle Brigade is a big commitment. Unlike some jobs that allow dogs to begin training with their owners, detector dog work requires the dog-in-training to start a whole new life. For this reason, most members of the Beagle Brigade are rescues, or dogs looking for a new home, like Tucker.

Every member of the Beagle Brigade is trained at the National Detector Dog Training Center in Georgia. Here the dogs have thirteen weeks to master their sniffing skills. Meanwhile, their handlers learn all about their canine partners. By the end of the program, not only does each dog need to identify the correct scents, each handler must know just what their partner is telling them. It's a tough process, and it's not for everyone. Dogs who don't make it through are matched with good homes and become pets. For teams that do make it through, they are assigned an airport and begin their important work.

At the age of nine, Beagle Brigade dogs retire. Most are adopted by their handlers, while others are found loving homes in which to live out their well-earned retirements.

Beagle

The beagle traces its history back to hare hunters of England from the 1500s. Today, their keen noses make them great working dogs, and their sunny attitudes make them the most popular hounds around.

Height and Weight: Under 13 inches, under 20 pounds; 13–15 inches, 20–30 pounds
Life Span: 10–15 years
Coat: Black, tan, and white
Known for: Friendliness, curiosity

Belgian Malinois

This breed was first brought to the United States to work as a police dog. Today, these hardworking dogs serve many roles, including TSA detector dog.

Height: 22–26 inches
Weight: 40–80 pounds
Life Span: 14–16 years
Coat: Brown, black, and tan
Known for: Confidence, smarts, strength

Breed information based on American Kennel Club data. For more on these and other breeds, visit www.akc.org/dog-breeds/.

🐾 Acknowledgments 🐾

I love to meet in real life the dogs with the big jobs that I write about. That proved a challenge for this book, however. During my research and writing for this title about a dog that works at an airport, much of the world was sheltering in place during the COVID-19 pandemic.

Fortunately, I was able to arrange a virtual, on-screen meeting with the wonderful Scottish rough collie Sir Duke, a member of the San Antonio International Airport's Pups and Planes volunteer therapy dog program, and I spoke by telephone with his very kind and proud people, Bill and Arlene Wimp.

Although the program had been temporarily put on hold due to safety restrictions, Bill and Arlene told me all about it and answered my many questions. They also shared heartwarming stories about Sir Duke's life and work with San Antonio's comfort/therapy dog organization, Paws for Service. I am so very grateful to them for sharing their knowledge and insights with me!

As always, much appreciation also to illustrator Francesca Rosa, editor Jonathan Westmark, and the whole AW team.